Learning to Read, Step by Step!

Ready to Read   Preschool–Kindergarten
• big type and easy words • rhyme and rhythm • picture clues
For children who know the alphabet and are eager to begin reading.

Reading with Help   Preschool–Grade 1
• basic vocabulary • short sentences • simple stories
For children who recognize familiar words and sound out new words with help.

Reading on Your Own   Grades 1–3
• engaging characters • easy-to-follow plots • popular topics
For children who are ready to read on their own.

Reading Paragraphs   Grades 2–3
• challenging vocabulary • short paragraphs • exciting stories
For newly independent readers who read simple sentences with confidence.

Ready for Chapters   Grades 2–4
• chapters • longer paragraphs • full-color art
For children who want to take the plunge into chapter books but still like colorful pictures.

STEP INTO READING® is designed to give every child a successful reading experience. The grade levels are only guides; children will progress through the steps at their own speed, developing confidence in their reading. The F&P Text Level on the back cover serves as another tool to help you choose the right book for your child.

Remember, a lifetime love of reading starts with a single step!

With special thanks to Richard Weston

To T-ball players everywhere,
and their dogs—play ball!
—T.P.

For my favorite grandson, Neil
—S.D.

Text copyright © 2018 by Terry Pierce
Cover art and interior illustrations copyright © 2018 by Sue DiCicco

All rights reserved. Published in the United States by Random House Children's Books,
a division of Penguin Random House LLC, New York.

Step into Reading, Random House, and the Random House colophon are registered trademarks
of Penguin Random House LLC.

Visit us on the Web!
StepIntoReading.com
rhcbooks.com

Educators and librarians, for a variety of teaching tools, visit us at RHTeachersLibrarians.com

Library of Congress Cataloging-in-Publication Data
Names: Pierce, Terry, author. | DiCicco, Sue, illustrator.
Title: Jack and Jill and T-Ball Bill / Terry Pierce ; illustrations, Sue DiCicco.
Description: First edition. | New York : Random House, [2018] | Series: Step into reading. Step 1|
Summary: Siblings Jack and Jill deal with their dog, Bill, interrupting their T-ball game.
Identifiers: LCCN 2016018412 (print) | LCCN 2016057338 (ebook) | ISBN 978-1-5247-1413-0 (pbk.)|
ISBN 978-1-5247-1414-7 (lib. bdg.) | ISBN 978-1-5247-1415-4 (ebook)
Subjects: | CYAC: Stories in rhyme. | Dogs—Fiction. | T-ball—Fiction. | Brothers and sisters—
Fiction.
Classification: LCC PZ8.3.P558643 Jac 2018 (print) | LCC PZ8.3.P558643 (ebook) | DDC [E]—dc23

Printed in the United States of America
10 9 8 7 6 5 4 3 2 1

First Edition

This book has been officially leveled by using the F&P Text Level Gradient™ Leveling System.

Jack and Jill and T-Ball Bill

by Terry Pierce
illustrated by Sue DiCicco

Random House New York

The game is on.
Batter up!

Pups play Jets.

Jack steps up.

He swings the bat.

Crack!

A hit!

The ball goes past
a red Jets mitt.

It rolls and rolls
out to the wall.

Big Bill runs out.

He grabs the ball!

Big Bill runs fast.

The Pups all call,

"Come back, Big Bill!

We need our ball!"

Pups and Jets
go after Bill.

They run.
They trip.

Here comes Jill!

Jill can run.

Bill can jump!

But stop?

Oh, no!

Here comes the ump!

His hands are out.

He tilts.

He tips.

Big Bill stops.

He dips.

He yips.

Bill plays a game
of keep-away.
He wants to run
and romp and play.

Jill needs a plan.

Think hard, Jill!

How can you get

that ball from Bill?

Bill cocks his head.

He looks around.

That is when

he hears a sound. . . .

"Hot dog! Hot dog!

Come and get it!"

Jill calls Bill.

He sees the snack.

Sniff, sniff!

Woof!

Bill runs back.

Bill licks his lips.

He gulps the snack.

Jill grabs the ball.

She throws to Jack.

The T-ball game
is back on track!

Next up to hit?

It is Jill.

She smacks the ball.

And there goes Bill!